2/08

DATE DUE

JUN 25 08			
JUL 07 '08			
JE 24 '1			
SE 0 7 1			
SE 23 1			
JA 17 3			
IY 2 0 1			

**Put Beginning Readers on the Right Track with
ALL ABOARD READING™**

The All Aboard Reading series is especially designed for beginning readers. Written by noted authors and illustrated in full color, these are books that children really want to read—books to excite their imagination, expand their interests, make them laugh, and support their feelings. With fiction and nonfiction stories that are high interest and curriculum-related, All Aboard Reading books offer something for every young reader. And with four different reading levels, the All Aboard Reading series lets you choose which books are most appropriate for your children and their growing abilities.

Picture Readers

Picture Readers have super-simple texts, with many nouns appearing as rebus pictures. At the end of each book are 24 flash cards—on one side is a rebus picture; on the other side is the written-out word.

Station Stop 1

Station Stop 1 books are best for children who have just begun to read. Simple words and big type make these early reading experiences more comfortable. Picture clues help children to figure out the words on the page. Lots of repetition throughout the text helps children to predict the next word or phrase—an essential step in developing word recognition.

Station Stop 2

Station Stop 2 books are written specifically for children who are reading with help. Short sentences make it easier for early readers to understand what they are reading. Simple plots and simple dialogue help children with reading comprehension.

Station Stop 3

Station Stop 3 books are perfect for children who are reading alone. With longer text and harder words, these books appeal to children who have mastered basic reading skills. More complex stories captivate children who are ready for more challenging books.

In addition to All Aboard Reading books, look for All Aboard Math Readers™ (fiction stories that teach math concepts children are learning in school) and All Aboard Science Readers™ (nonfiction books that explore the most fascinating science topics in age-appropriate language).

All Aboard for happy reading!

To David who always helps with
the math homework!—B.B.

For Glenna and Ian—M.G.C.

Text copyright © 2003 by Bonnie Bader. Illustrations copyright © 2003 by Mernie
Gallagher Cole. All rights reserved. Published by Grosset & Dunlap, a division of
Penguin Young Readers Group, 345 Hudson Street, New York, NY 10014. GROSSET
& DUNLAP and ALL ABOARD MATH READER are trademarks of Penguin Group
(USA) Inc. Published simultaneously in Canada. Printed in the U.S.A.

Library of Congress Cataloging-in-Publication Data is available.

ISBN 0-448-42896-2 (pbk)   B C D E F G H I J

ISBN 0-448-43237-4 (GB)   A B C D E F G H I J

ALL ABOARD MATH READER™ — Station Stop 2

GRAPHS

By Bonnie Bader
Illustrated by Mernie Gallagher Cole

Grosset & Dunlap • New York

"Time to get up!" my mom called.
I looked at the clock. It read 7:00.
There must be some mistake, I
thought. It was Saturday morning.
I had no school today.

"Come on, Gary," my mom said.

I turned over. I pulled the pillow over my head.

"Get out of bed. Now."

She sounded serious. I pulled the pillow off my face. I opened one eye. "Why so early?" I whispered.

"Don't you remember?" my mom said. "Today's our family reunion."

"Umph!" I muttered. I pulled the covers over my head.

"Let's go," my mom said. She pulled the covers off my head. "We're leaving in half an hour."

I knew I had to think fast. There was no way I was going to suffer through another Graff Family Reunion.

"I-I have to stay home and clean out my closet," I said.

"Nice try," my mom said with a smile. "I cleaned out your closet last week."

"Um, um, I have to stay home and do laundry," I said.

Mom shook her head. She held out a clean pair of shorts and a T-shirt for me to wear.

"I-I have to stay home and do my math homework," I said.

Mom was quiet. It looked like she was thinking about it. Maybe that excuse would work.

"You can bring your math homework with you," my mom told me. "I'm sure Aunt Molly will have a table you can use to work on."

Rats! I guess I had no choice but to go.

After a very long car ride, we finally arrived at Aunt Molly Graff's house. Most of the Graff family was already there.

"Oh, look how much you have grown!" Aunt Molly said as she gave my right cheek a big pinch.

"Oh, you look just like your father!"
Aunt Sadie said as she gave my left cheek
an even bigger pinch.

"Oh, no, I think you look just like your
mother!" Aunt Jenny said. I ducked before
she could find something else to pinch.

There was no way I was going to stand around getting pinched all day.

"Um, Mom," I said. "Homework time."

She gave me a nod. I made my move.

I went inside to
find an empty room.
Uncle Stanley was
sleeping in the family
room. Too noisy.

My cousins were
playing dolls in the
living room.
Too girly.

Little Allie was
getting her diaper
changed in the
bedroom. Too stinky.

I went outside again.
Maybe I could find a
tree to sit under.

Yes! I found a tree.
There was shade.
And there was no one
around.

I sat down and pulled out my math
book.

I had to make at least three different
graphs. A bar graph. A line graph. A pie
graph.

What in the world was I going to graph?
I lay back on the grass to think.

Just then I heard voices. It sounded
like Aunt Molly and Aunt Sadie were
arguing. I opened one eye to spy.

"It's going to be at least one hundred
degrees today!" Aunt Molly said.
"All my food will spoil!"

"Oh Molly, you always worry.
I don't think we'll break ninety degrees
today," Aunt Sadie said.

"Ninety will be just as bad!" Aunt Molly shouted. "Look at the time. It's only eleven o'clock. And it's already eighty-eight degrees. By noon it'll be ninety-two for sure!" And with that, Aunt Molly stormed away.

I bolted up. I had just gotten an idea for my first graph. I would chart the temperature and the time.

I got to work.

I had just started plotting my graph when Aunt Sadie spotted me.

"Gary!" she cried. "Why are you sitting there all by yourself? Go join the rest of the family!"

"But, I . . ." I began.

"No buts," Aunt Sadie said. "This is a party. Now go join the fun. Shoo! Shoo!"

I got going.

I didn't get very far before Aunt Molly caught me. She did not look happy.

"Gary," she said. "It's time to eat."

I looked at my watch. It was not lunchtime.

"But it's too early for lunch," I said.

"Well, we all have to start eating now," Aunt Molly said. "It's going to be a hot one today, and I don't want my food to spoil."

20

I did not want to argue with her.
Then she grabbed me. Oh no, I
thought. Here comes another pinch.
Instead of a pinch, Aunt Molly just
pulled me close and whispered in my ear,
"Be sure to try some of my homemade
potato salad. It's better than Aunt Sadie's
coleslaw. She bought it at the store!"

I wasn't hungry. But I had another idea.
When no one was looking, I slipped under
the salad table. I pulled out some paper.
And some sharpened pencils.
I waited. And I watched.

   Five aunts took the potato salad.
So did my mom.

   Six cousins took the macaroni salad.
So did three uncles. And my dad.

And two aunts, four cousins, and eight uncles piled their plates with coleslaw. My grandma and grandpa took some, too.

I waited a while longer. But there were no more takers.

My bar graph was done. The coleslaw was the clear favorite.

I would make sure not to tell Aunt Molly.

My stomach started to growl.
I looked at my watch. It was 1:00.
My stomach would have to wait.

I raced over to the thermometer. It read 93 degrees.

I marked the temperature on my graph.

I walked over to the food tables.

I piled my plate high.

I picked up a knife and a fork.

But there weren't any napkins.

I looked around at my family.
A few people had napkins.
But most didn't.
I got another idea for a graph.

I quickly ate my lunch.
Then I started to walk
around with my notebook.
I counted ten people
using napkins.

I counted thirteen
people using their
sleeves.

And I counted twenty-two people using the back of their hands!

Yuck!

But at least another graph was done!

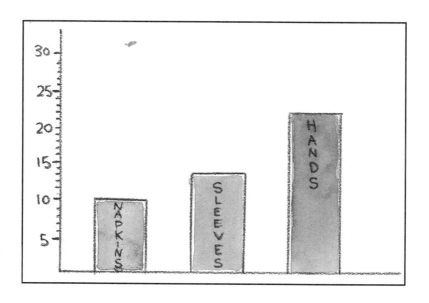

As I looked around for something else to do, a girl came up to me.

She had red hair and blue eyes.

"Hi!" she said. "I'm Becky. I think we're related."

"Of course we are," I told her. "That's why we're all here."

"Do you want to play?" Becky asked me.
I looked at my watch. It was 2:00.
"Sorry," I told her. "I have things to do."

I walked over to the thermometer.

It read 95 degrees.

I made a mark on my graph.

When I was done, I looked up. Becky
was standing there. A boy was standing
next to her. He looked just like her. Same
hair. Same eyes. Same height.

"This is my brother, Bobby," Becky
told me. "We're twins."

"I can see that," I said.

"Want to play?" Bobby asked.

"Sorry," I said. "I have work to do."

I started to walk away.

Becky and Bobby followed me.

"What kind of work?" Becky wanted to know.

I told them about my math homework.
I thought they would be bored by it and
leave me alone.

I was wrong.

"Cool!" said Becky.

"We love math!" said Bobby. "Can we help? This reunion is pretty boring."

"I guess," I said. "But only if you can think of something to graph."

"How about hair color?" Becky asked. "I think there are more redheads here than anything else."

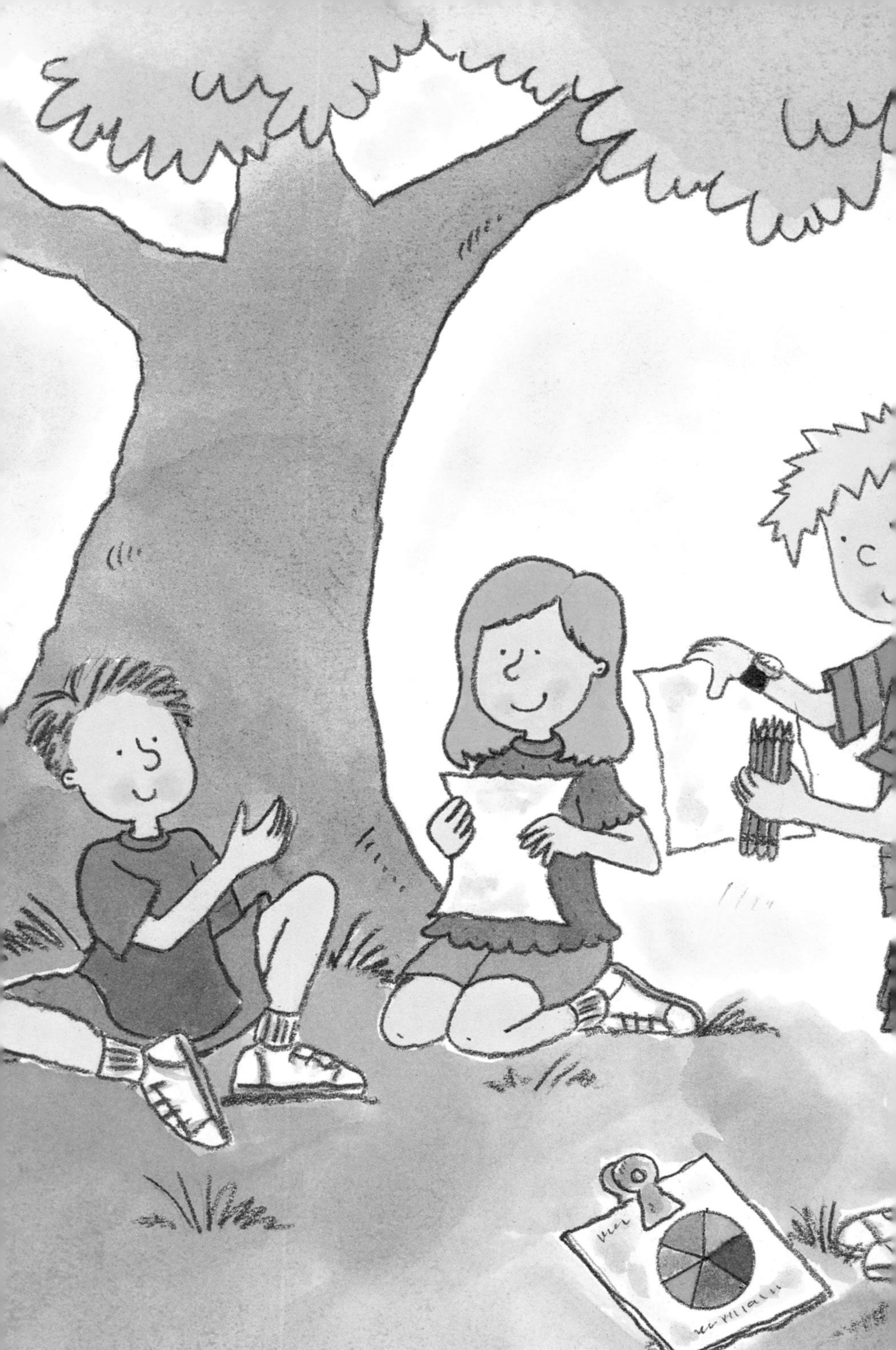

I thought a minute.

Then I handed Becky and Bobby some paper.

"Okay," I said. "Becky, you count the people with red hair. Bobby, you do brown. I'll do blond and other."

"Other?" Becky and Bobby said together.

"You'll see," I said with a smile. "Now, shoo! Shoo!"

Yikes! I was starting to sound like Aunt Sadie!

We met up a little while later.

Bobby had counted people with
brown hair.

Becky had counted people with
red hair.

And I had counted people with
blond hair.

And people with no hair.

"Oh, so that was the other!" Bobby said.

"I thought the other was going to be gray hair," Becky said.

I looked around. There were no people with gray hair. "That's strange," I said. "There are some old people here, but no one has gray hair."

Blond 卌 𝙸𝙸𝙸
Bald 卌
Brown 卌 𝙸𝙸𝙸
Red 卌

"You're right," Bobby said.

"Maybe if we get up real close to them we can find out their real hair color," Becky suggested.

Just then, two more kids walked up to us.

"Hi! I'm Sally, and this is my brother Sammy. What are you guys doing?"

I filled them in on my math project.

"Cool," said Sally.

"Supercool," said Sammy.

Cool. That reminded me that I had to check the temperature.

I excused myself and made another mark on my graph.

As I was heading back, my cousins were nowhere in sight.

I looked around. Bobby was giving Aunt Jenny a kiss.

Becky was giving Aunt Sadie a hug.

Sally was sitting
on Uncle Max's lap.
And Sammy was
letting Aunt Molly
give him a pinch.

We now had four gray-haired people.
I fixed my data. My graphs were done.

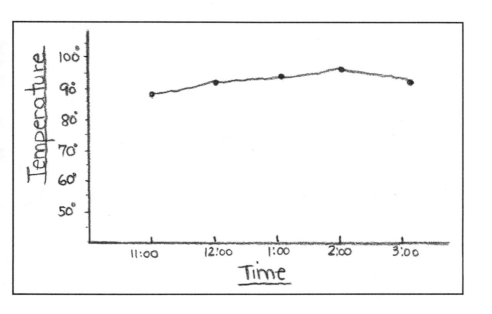

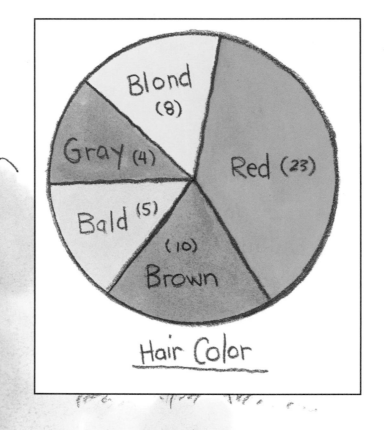

Hair Color

"Time to go home, Gary!" my mom called.

"So soon?" I asked.

My mom gave me a strange look. "You mean you had fun?" she asked.

I smiled. I said good-bye to my cousins. We made plans to see one another soon. This family reunion wasn't so bad after all.

Plus, I got my math homework done!